DRAGON KNIGHT

SIR PATRICK BIJOU

BOOK DESCRIPTION

iii

From bestselling author Sir Patrick Bijou comes an erotic and enthralling reimagining of the knight, Varyn, summoned by a pretty young priestess Allorah after the invaders from the island's northern shore attacked the village.

Day by day, heavy war from invaders from the north and the death toll rose. They had landed on the island's northern shore when she was still just a child, and they brought with them bizarre creatures, and unfamiliar ways.

A genuinely infectious state of eroticism captures the imagination that awaits in this spine-chilling erotic suspense thriller.

ABOUT THE AUTHOR

Sir Patrick lives and writes in the United Kingdom and is the author of several books on finance and fiction. He is known for his extraordinary skills in settling and negotiating peace settlements and international law and is a prodigious legal and political adviser. His diverse writing ability has been influenced by many experiences, making him the success he is today.

He has written many books and articles about the liberation of people, highlighting the issues of those whom the literary world of creative writing has not enlightened. His voyage into content writing has made him a remarkably inspired author and professional communicator.

Sir Patrick has written over 37 none fictional and fictional books spanning several genres.

To find out more about Sir Patrick Bijou visit his website

www.sirpatrickbijou.com
www.bijouebook.com

TABLE OF CONTENTS

CHAPTER 1

Violent winds whipped the trees into a frenzied dance, shaking free debris and leaves that swept down from the forest's edge to swirl around the young woman standing alone on the beach. Allorah looked at the bruised clouds with trepidation. Dark and heavy, they crouched on the horizon, illuminated every few minutes by wicked spikes of lightning. Bone-shaking growls of thunder were amplified by the black expanse of the ocean until they seemed nearly deafening to the inhabitants of the small island. Never in her lifetime had there been such a storm, yet she had the foreboding sense that this was only a precursor to the actual threat.

The threat was posed by the invaders to the north.

Tall and strange, they had landed on the island's northern shore when she was still just a child, and they brought with them bizarre creatures and unfamiliar ways. Almost as soon as they had arrived, they began clearing the woods around their landing area, erecting houses and fences with the raw wood, and set loose their animals to graze on the newly opened spaces. To her people, who lived in the sheltering boughs of the trees, such behavior was unfathomable and unnerving. Especially when rumors of what had happened to the original inhabitants of the northern region began to circulate. Soon after, it was decided that everyone would withdraw to the south, and there they remained for twelve years. No one ventured to the north, and the foreigners didn't seem interested in probing farther than a mile from their settlement.

Until a year ago.

Perhaps their population had reached a size where expansion was becoming necessary, or maybe their youths were frustrated with the confines of their territory. Whatever the reason, they had begun making expeditions into her people's land, and the encounters between the two were increasingly violent. Events came to a head at a time when Allorah was spending a rare night among the other people of her town.

People sat around the communal fire, talking, eating, and singing in the company of their fellows. Women shared gossip and news, older men told circles of children about some of their more exciting hunting experiences, and young men vied for the attention of the maidens, that giggled and blushed in response. Since the communal fire was one of the few things to be located on the forest floor —as all but small cook-fires posed a hazard to the wooden structures of their arboreal homes— nearly the entire village could gather around the cheerful blaze.

Allorah sat to the side, not completely alone. A few bolder youths had positioned themselves around her and attempted to coax her into a conversation. One boy, in particular, Geldan, was incredibly persistent. He was only two years older than she but was already decorated as one of the town's finest hunters. She saw how the eyes of the town maidens followed him, watching the muscular lines of his sun-browned body, and she knew any of them would count themselves lucky to be in her place.

Yet the attention made her uncomfortable. She was apprenticed to the island's Priestess, and though her vows did not constrain her to celibacy, her training kept her mostly in solitude with the older woman as her only companion. In fact, up until her fifteenth year, the only people she had seen at all, aside from those she and the Priestess were called upon to heal, were her parents, and then only on rare occasions. At that time, Priestess Dannonae must have felt it was time to begin re-introducing her to society, so they started making trips from their secluded tower home to the complicated network of walkways and bridges of the town. It was then, Allorah believed, that Geldan had first taken an interest in her. On each of their visits after that, he always seemed to find ways to cross paths with her, and she could feel his gaze on her as she went about her business.

Sitting by the fire, she listened politely to his stories but never allowed herself to be fully drawn into the discourse. He didn't stop trying, though. Not until the wounded boy staggered into the clearing.

There was a collective gasp, then a swirl of activity as people rushed to the boy's side, and others ran to fetch healing items. They quickly made room for Dannonae and Allorah, for they were the most skilled healers on the island, yet as soon as Allorah saw him, she knew his wounds were fatal.

He was bleeding from multiple places on his body, but the killing blow was a horrible gash in his belly, barely held together by his weakening hand. Priestess Dannonae knelt at his head, cradling it, and Allorah moved to his side to keep his free hand. They remained like that as he used his dying breath to tell them what had happened:

He had been a member of a small hunting party that had the misfortune to cross paths with a wandering group of foreigners. Many of them were cut down within minutes, but the boy and a few others had managed to escape, fleeing back to what he thought was the safety of his village. Suffice it to say, he was followed. Next was a merciless slaughter of all the menfolk, and while the boy hid and watched, the foreigners proceeded to loot what little the village had in goods. They grew heartily drunk and made games of raping the women. The children soon grew tired, so they slit their throats and carried on with their activities. At some point, the boy's hiding place was discovered, and it was then he obtained the wounds he would die from. They were too drunk to finish the job, however, and the boy fled again, somehow managing to make it to where he now lay, passing along his horrifying tale through lips increasingly frothed with blood.

There was a stunned silence after he had finished. Hushed murmuring began again as a few people returned with the healing things, and Dannonae quickly recruited several men to lift and carry the boy to a more isolated location. Allorah followed, and when they placed him in a small room on a level close the the forest floor, she and the

Priestess went about trying to make him as comfortable as possible for the little time he had left.

After a few minutes, shouting erupted from the area around the communal fire. Affirming that Allorah could take care of matters with the boy, Dannonae returned to the fire to oversee the inevitable debate that was taking place there. As she sat, gently stroking the boy's hair back from his face and holding his hand, Allorah listened to the heated voices outside. They rose and fell in anxious rhythms, but she could not make out more than the occasional word. It was hours later, when the moon had set, and the boy rested in a state of unconsciousness that he would never wake from, that Dannonae finally returned. She wearily brushed a hand across her face, looking grimmer than Allorah had ever seen her.

"What has happened?" She asked. Dannonae sighed and closed her eyes for a moment.

"There still needs to be a complete gathering of all the village Heads before we can come to an official decision, but that is only a formality. The events we heard described tonight prove what I long knew -and dreaded- would come to pass. There is only one course of action for such a thing, and they all know it. It was only a matter of time..." She trailed off, lost in her thoughts.

Allorah rose from her bedside post and went to Dannonae. She shook her gently, trying to draw her back to reality. "What was only a matter of time, Mother? What?" Allorah felt an ominous dread in the pit of her own stomach, at once needing to know the answer and fearing to hear it.

Dannonae gave a tired sigh and placed one hand gently on the crown of Allorah's head. Suddenly, she looked ancient. Her white hair hung in despondent wisps around her face, and the lines around her grey eyes seemed to have deepened over the course of the night. Allorah stood still and waited. The answer, when it came, shook her to her very core.

"My dearest child, we are going to war."

And war it was. It was only a matter of hearing the boy's story to convince the other village Heads, and his tattered young corpse was enough proof for anyone of the story's authenticity. For the past year, hunters from each of the scattered villages had taken up arms against the invaders from the north, and most proved to be as apt at hunting men as they had been at hunting beasts. However, the foreigners soon took note of her people's new temperament, and they increased their own aggression in response. Her people fought their best, and they used every advantage their familiarity with the land could afford them, but it soon became apparent that this was not enough. It was all they could do to slow the foreigners' relentless advance south, and the death toll increased daily. There were simply too many of them, and her people had never been conditioned to war as these strangers seemed to be.

For Allorah, it was particularly frustrating. She and the Priestess worked until exhaustion to deal with the steady stream of wounded men and boys that came back from the front lines. Yet, they were only two, and they could only help to mend that which had already been broken, never able to take more direct action. Allorah knew that unless something happened to change the tide of the war, her people would eventually fall.

On the eve of her eighteenth birthday, a tremendous battle was fought alarmingly close to one of the island's main villages. Their forces emerged victorious, but only just, and Allorah spent the entire night and most of the next day tending to the injured. In a rare moment of calm, Allorah was startled to see Dannonae approach her with an ancient-looking scroll in hand. The Priestess would not explain her motivation, saying only that Allorah should read it. She did.

It was instructions for a ritual, and it contained an unfamiliar version of an old myth Allorah had been told when she was small. The essence was that in a time of great peril, the inhabitants of her island had somehow managed to bridge the gap between their world and the Other, the realm of dragon warriors. They had enlisted the help of several of these fierce denizens and, through their efforts, had triumphed over the evil that plagued their land. It was a common story and one of Allorah's favorites, but the scroll seemed to suggest that, impossibly, the tale was more than mere myth.

In confusion, she went to Dannonae and insisted that she explain.

"My dear, you know as well as I that we cannot continue like this. We must either seek help, or we will be overrun."

"Help? Help from whom?" Allorah paced the room, too tired to sit still. "Priestess, I don't understand. What does this scroll have to do with the war?"

"Everything. The ritual contained therein is the key to our survival." Dannonae watched her restless movements with an Elder's calm. As Allorah opened her mouth to ask another question, Dannonae silenced her with a raised hand. "We haven't the time for me to explain all, but I will tell you this: the rite is a spell of Summoning."

"A Summoning..." Allorah breathed. Though she had heard of such a spell, once again, it had only been as a children's tale. According to legend, a Summoning opened the magical Gates between worlds and, as the name suggested, summoned a creature to their own world. In the past, it had been performed in times of need, but as peace settled firmly over the island, the knowledge of how to invoke it had been lost. Suddenly, Allorah understood.

Dannonae watched realization dawn. "Yes, my child. It is our only chance."

Allorah nodded, determination set in. "Then we must begin preparations immediately; we've no time to waste." She quickly strode over to where the scroll rested on a counter and scooped it up, scanning its contents hurriedly. "It says we will need to gather..." She trailed off when she noticed the Priestess had not moved.

"There will be no 'we' this time, Allorah. This is something you must do. Alone."

"But... Mother, I am only an apprentice." She said in confusion. "Surely this is something for a full Priestess—"

"You are a priestess in all but name, Allorah, and you know it," Dannonae said, cutting her off. "If not for this war, we would have already held the official ceremony." Seeing the expression of shocked doubt Allorah wore, she continued in a gentler tone. "You have all the tools you will need for this. Trust yourself."

She shook her head. "I don't think I can do this. Too much depends on it. Couldn't you—?"

"No." Dannonae said sharply. "It must be you. I can't say why just that... Just that I am not fit for it. It must be you."

Allorah felt a wave of doubt threaten to overwhelm her, but she knew the old Priestess well enough to tell when she'd dug her heels in. She closed her eyes and took a deep, shuddering breath to muster her courage for the task ahead. It took two more similar breaths until she was ready to open her eyes again. "I supposed I had better get working, then."

"Yes," Dannonae agreed, "for the ritual must be performed tonight."

She spent the rest of the day collecting the things she would need. Various herbs, a ceremonial knife, candles, a skin from one of the giant cats that resided on the island, mortar and pestle, logs for the fire, and of course, the scroll. The ritual was surprisingly simple, and for that, Allorah was grateful. She was not sure she could manage something more complicated in her exhaustion.

The lightning crackled, rousing her from her thoughts. She spent one more moment staring out at the darkened ocean as the gale made her midnight hair dance around her delicate face. She pressed the nearly transparent ceremonial robe close to her body before she pivoted and walked back to the forest. As soon as she'd reached the shelter of the tree line, the wind lessened considerably, but she still found herself wishing that she'd had the foresight to bring a cloak or a shawl to keep in the heat her thin garment did not.

Still, as she made her way through the darkened forest on silent feet, the movement restored some measure of warmth to her, and the act of focusing on where she stepped kept her alert. She needed fear no foreigners here in the heart of the wooded island, but though she knew these lands so well as to be able to navigate them blindfolded, it seemed irreverent to disturb the soothing quiet that pervaded this sacred place. And walking without sound, in the pitch black of the moonless night, required concentration.

The subtle aura of ancient power that pervaded part of the island seemed to thrum through the trees around her, the stream she followed, and the earth itself, rising through the soles of her bare feet to resonate with the echoes of her heartbeat. She could feel the soul of this place, slow and sure and still so powerful, even after ages had passed. Allorah felt herself being pulled gently into a dream-like state. Awake, but not.

For a moment, it was as if she looked through the eyes of another, seeing herself from the outside: the pure white of flowing robe and the porcelain of skin stood out in the blackness, ethereal and ghostly. She noticed, with mild embarrassment, that the garment did little to hide the contours of her young body. Narrow shoulders tapered to a tiny waist, flaring again at her hips to give way to shapely legs that were long in proportion to the rest of her slim body. Her breasts, round and firm, were not as large as some but still had weight enough to bounce softly as she walked, the plain robe doing more in the way of draping than supporting. Thankfully, the sash that kept the garment closed hung down at the front, obscuring the black thatch of hair at the junction of her legs that Allorah was certain would otherwise be visible through the scanty material. At her shoulders, her long raven's-wing hair fell in soft waves. In daylight, the sun reflected silver on its silken length. Still, under the midnight trees, the obsidian tresses blended eerily with the background, adding to the image of some otherworldly being. And then there were her eyes. In that instant of strange vision, her eyes, an unusual violet shade under normal circumstances, seemed to glow with some internal light.

The vision vanished as she reached her destination, but she remained in a state of half-dream as she began the ritual. She quickly kindled a fire in the center of the ancient glade, in a pit designed for that purpose that looked like it hadn't been used in decades. She laid out the cat skin in front of it and made careful designs on the surrounding earth with candle wax. It was slow, tedious work, but she was patient, and eventually, that step was complete upon placing the candles at precise locations of the pattern. Next, she seated herself on the skin, opened several bags of the herbs she had collected, and began mixing and grinding them in the mortar. When she finished, she picked up the knife. It was a simple thing, unadorned except for a tiny circle engraved on the base of the blade. Murmuring the required words, she made a quick, shallow cut on her thumb and let five drops fall into the herb mixture. She carefully set the knife aside.

Finally, she stood, removing all the tools of her preparation from the skin, and untied the sash of her robe. Without it, the fine cloth fell open, slithering from her shoulders to pool on the ground at her feet. She folded it neatly and set that aside as well. Then she knelt and took three deep breaths. Everything was ready.

The incantation in the scroll came quickly to her lips; she'd taken the time earlier in the day to memorize it, leaving her free to focus. Like the rest of the ritual, it was elegantly simple, a short phrase of words laden with power. As she spoke them repeatedly, she occasionally took a pinch of the herb and blood mixture, tossing it into the fire. It flared dramatically, each time causing the fire to swell in size until it was a massive blaze.

Allorah could sense the energy of the land and spell gathering and building and became distantly aware that the flames had changed in color from orange to a bluish-white. She felt more than heard a low rumble around her. It, too, began to change, rising in pitch until it was a shrilling whine, seeming to swirl around her like the wailing of malevolent spirits. For a moment, Allorah's steady chanting faltered as the sound pierced her concentration, but she quickly refocused herself and continued, raising her voice to match the volume of the roar.

Just as she was sure she could not endure it any longer, the sound abruptly ceased, and she was left shouting to the still night. She drew slow, shuddering breaths, waiting for something to happen. Only silence. Then, suddenly, she realized what she needed to do, and the words came to her from someplace deep within.

"Warrior, our need is great; I summon thee from beyond the Gate!"

And, so saying, she threw all the rest of the herbal mixture into the fire.

A loud boom and a flash of light so brilliant it was blinding. Allorah felt it knocked backward from the force of the explosion, and for several moments, she could only lay there. When she gathered the strength to push herself upright again, her eyes went immediately to the fire. At its center, there seemed to be something forming. A shape grew out of the conflagration, solidifying into the form of a man.

He stepped from the flame, and she was dazzled by his radiance. She was unsure what she had been expecting; an enormous dragon, perhaps, or some human-beast hybrid. Indeed not the long-limbed god she saw before her. There was no clothing to hide the sculpted beauty of his body, the perfect breadth of his shoulders tapering to slim hips. His emerald eyes took in her own unclothed body, roaming over her, assessing her. "You are the one that summoned me?" His voice was deep and powerful. Allorah could only nod in awe. He advanced slowly, his eyes never leaving her. She felt a stirring of something within her and undefined yearning, a needing. The light danced over the hardened muscles of his chest and arms and the silver spikes of his hair. He knelt on one knee before her.

"I am the Warrior Varyn. I am here to serve." He said formally, then paused. His tone changed. "What is your name?"

"Allorah," she breathed. His intense green eyes mesmerized her. The yearning inside her had grown and changed into something stronger. She could feel a strange and unfamiliar sensation between her legs.

"Allorah," he whispered, "Beautiful."

His hand reached out, tracing her cheek and her trembling lips. Her body quivered in excitement as that hand dropped down to tweak her rose-colored nipple casually. Alien passion roared through her small frame, crying out for her to return the touch, but inexperience and nervousness kept her immobile. Varyn paused, watching her expression, then he moved for her.

Her head swam as he enveloped her mouth in a hungry, insistent kiss. His tongue plunged inward, exploring, claiming, and she tugged and bit at his lower lip in response. Part of her was shocked by the sudden boldness but soon swept away in the tide of desire flooding her senses. She had never done anything even close to this before, but right now, she didn't care. In this place of half-dream, it just seemed right.

Somehow, she was lying on her back, and he was kissing his way down her body. Nipping and licking her jaw, ear, neck, and collarbone. He was deterred by the twin peaks of her breasts, so he stopped his downward journey to circle them with his tongue, one at a time. His lips enveloped her left nipple. He pulled it into his mouth, flicking it with his tongue and raking it with his teeth, almost to the point of pain. Allorah moaned, her hands tightening on his solid shoulders. Switching to her right breast, he suckled and nibbled while his hands roamed down her body. She shivered as his lips traced her flat belly, and those strong hands crept up the insides of her thighs.

When his mouth finally reached her most private places, she gasped in surprise and delight. She'd never felt anything so sweet, so agonizingly pleasurable. His tongue ran over her nether- lips, then unexpectedly plunged inside her, and she cried out at the sensations flooding her body. Before long, his tongue moved slightly to tease her innocent bud, and something much harder and longer found its way to her entrance. She whimpered as he penetrated her with his finger. Nothing had ever been inside her before, and the sudden intrusion was not entirely comfortable. She could feel it bumping up against her maidenhead. But as he began to work it in and out of her, she could feel herself lubricating it, and soon the frantic activity of his tongue had her panting with desire. When he inserted a second finger, she could only moan.

Suddenly it stopped, and she opened her eyes, not even remembering when she'd closed them, to find Varyn crawling up toward her again. His body forced her legs further apart, and she could feel his enormous erection pushing against her untried entrance. The lust apparent in his hardness was echoed in his eyes and her own heart.

"Please," she gasped.

He silenced her scream of pain with his mouth as he forced himself into her with one brutal thrust. She could feel delicate tissue stretch and rip open. It was as if the action released something wild within him, and suddenly there was a different man on top of her. Any semblance of gentleness was gone; he drove himself into her with merciless savagery, conquering her tight, virginal body violently and cruelly. His monstrous cock plunged in and out of her, stained with blood, pulling nearly the entire way out before he shoved it back inside, even deeper than before. Her only blessing was the plentiful juices that eased its passage somewhat. Her own juices she could taste on his lips as he muffled her continuing cries with bruising kisses.

Allorah thought she might faint with the pain, that it might be a blessing if she did. But then, unbelievably, her body began to respond. The tremendous cock that she would have trouble wrapping her hand around was hitting someplace deep within her, sending electric thrills through her whole body. At the same time, he had her stretched so far open that her tiny button rubbed against the base of his tool every time he thrust in. She dimly heard her cries of pain turn to wild pleasure, and she squirmed beneath him, twisting against the rock-hard pole that filled her so completely, shoving her hips up to meet each thrust in an attempt to capture more of him inside her.

"More," she panted against his lips. She could feel the heat building, the climax nearing. "Oh, please, more!"

He stared into her eyes as he obeyed. He thrust himself into her faster and even more deeply, penetrating her with such force that he slammed her whole body into the ground with every stroke. Shock waves shook her breasts in time with their coupling, making her hardened nipples brush against his muscular chest, slick with sweat. His breath came harshly, and beads of sweat grew on his face. She clung to him tighter, wrapping her legs around him and digging her heels into his backside. Still, he shoved into her viciously, relentlessly, and deeply.

"Oh, yes. Gods, yes, yes..."

He pushed, stabbed, and impaled her to her very heart until, at last, she felt her inner walls constrict in a vice-like grip around his cock, and her whole body tightened as she screamed her release to the night. Her pussy rippled in ecstasy, milking and massaging the length of him until she felt him drive himself inside her and hold, while powerful spasms sent thick ropes of his seed to fill her even more thoroughly. He grunted and quivered on top of her.

When her last shudder of orgasm finally passed, he slowly lowered himself to the ground next to her but remained skin-to-skin, still enveloped in her pussy and embrace. Their hands traced sweet patterns across each other's skin as they stared long at one another, but they did not speak. The talk was during the daylight hours. At last, Allorah felt herself drifting into slumber, safe and sated in the arms of her Warrior-lover from beyond the Gates.

Allorah awoke to the vigorous chirping of birds and an unfamiliar ache. It encompassed most of her belly but seemed to originate at the apex of her legs. Keeping her eyes tightly shut, she turned a little and burrowed deeper into the warm softness of her blankets. She knew she would have to deal with the bleeding soon enough, but in this chaotic time, quiet moments were rare, and she relished the opportunity to relax. When Dannonae came to wake her, she would get up.

At the thought of Dannonae, she sighed. The old Priestess had likely been up all night again, caring for the wounded. And as much as she wanted to stay abed, Allorah couldn't reconcile her own selfish wishes with the suffering of the men awaiting her attention. Reluctantly, she opened her eyes.

She noticed immediately that she was not in her bed. Instead, she was outdoors, in an ancient glade with the pale morning sun angling into light the area in sparkling rays. And she was not alone. A man sat near, cross-legged, studying her with brilliant green eyes. He was completely nude.

With a gasp of shock, Allorah shot upright, reaching too late for the cat skin that had been covering her as it fell to her waist. For a moment, she froze until she saw the man's lips curve in a small smile at the sight of her bare breasts, nipples proudly erect in the sudden draft. Her face burned in humiliation, and she quickly snatched up the pelt again to hold it close under her chin.

"Good morning, Priestess."

His voice sent shivers over her skin and suddenly unlocked her memories of the past night. She felt her cheeks flame brighter as she remembered the intimacy of those events and the reason why she was here now, naked, with this strange man.

"Warrior Varyn." She acknowledged curtly.

The more she remembered, the more she wished she didn't. Her behavior, her forwardness, was better suited to some twitterpated young goose than the apprentice of the Priestess! She had not known the man for two minutes, yet she had given herself to him. Completely. Without thought. What was wrong with her?

"I was beginning to think I would have to wake you." He said. "Yet you slept so sweetly; it seemed a shame."

"Yes, well, I was tired." She muttered, shrugging her ivory shoulders uncomfortably.

He grinned. "I can't imagine why."

She felt her blush deepen even further, but she straightened her back indignantly. "We Healers on this island have been hard-pressed over the past year, particularly these last few days. One rarely has the luxury of sleep anymore."

"Ahh..." He said, leaning forward intently. "And that is because you are at war, yes?" She nodded slowly and noted how his emerald eyes took on a predatory gleam. "Which is why you summoned me."

"Yes." She agreed. "You are a dragon warrior, born to fight. To one such as you, battling is as natural as breathing. Is this not so?"

He leaned back to rest on his elbows, stretching one leg casually. "My kind are rather good at killing, yes." His tone was also casual, but the predator's gleam was still in his eyes, and even relaxed, he radiated power. To Allorah he seemed like one of the giant island cats, a mass of sleek muscle and dangerous intelligence.

"Well, unfortunately, my people are not so gifted." She smiled bitterly. "We are being overrun."

"And you think I can change that?" He asked. There was no apparent malice in his voice, just curiosity.

Allorah cast her eyes down and shook her head. Ebony curls tumbled about her face. "I don't know what to think, Warrior. I can merely hope."

He didn't reply aloud, but Allorah could feel his eyes on her. They burned into her skin and made her shift uncomfortably, all too aware of how exposed she was. She felt very vulnerable and still terribly confused about what had made her act so rashly last night. It was true he possessed an Otherworldly attractiveness, but she had seen handsome men before, and she had not immediately gone to bed with them! Last night, it had almost been as if another person was acting from her body or as if she had been somehow bewitched...

That was it! Her violet eyes widened slightly, and she sucked in a sharp breath. She had been under the influence of the spell! Allorah remembered the sensation of half-dreaming, and now she recognized it for what it was: an enchantment.

She suddenly felt betrayed by her senses that succumbed so quickly to the deception, and Dannonae, who let her perform the ritual in ignorance. She felt her throat tighten with tears she would not allow herself to shed in front of Varyn. He lounged so casually in front of her, studying her quizzically. He who had taken her innocence. She needed to get away from him for a little while until she could compose herself.

Keeping the pelt covering her, she stood with some difficulty. Varyn stood too.

"No." She said, shaking her head. "You stay here."

He raised one silver eyebrow. "You're going somewhere?"

"I..." She cast about for a reasonable excuse. "I'm just going to wash up. In a stream nearby. I won't be long, and then I will tell you all I know about the invaders." She promised.

He shrugged. "All right." But he remained standing.

Allorah decided to do her business anyway and began looking for her robe. She spotted it quickly, off to the side where she'd left it, and picked it up. To put it on without relinquishing her meager covering was a more difficult task. Realizing it would look far more ridiculous to attempt to keep herself wholly covered throughout the process and be unwilling to bring more attention to the situation by asking Varyn to turn around. She dropped the pelt and hastily whipped the robe around her, turning away from him. She caught a glimpse of his expression before turning: a cat-like smile. It was enough to hurry her out.

As she'd said, the stream was not far, within hearing range of the ceremonial glade. A small waterfall sluiced into a quiet pool, with several moss-covered rocks that made excellent seats. Ferns surrounded it, but the trees were not packed so tightly here as to keep the place in the shadow. Instead, the sunlight filtered gently in, heating the water to bearable temperatures.

Allorah quickly stripped and waded in. The water was cold but not frigid, and soon she was into her thighs. Experience of the treacherousness of the weed-slick stones under her feet made her keep her balance against one of the larger rocks.

She washed quickly, pausing only once when she noted the dried blood on her inner thighs. As the water faded pink, she felt her throat tighten again, but she swallowed the lump and continued her ablutions. To wash her hair, she went to the waterfall and stood under the small protruding lip, letting the steady deluge pour over her. She closed her eyes and imagined the chilled water washing away her tension. The cold raised goose-flesh all over her ivory skin and made her small nipples into hard points, but she stayed under the stream for a long time.

When she finally emerged, she felt calm, serene as she had not in a great while. The feeling evaporated as she noticed Varyn standing on the bank.

He was different in the daylight. More alien. More commanding. The so-rare silver of his strangely spiked hair reflected the light, turning it to a bright corona that illuminated the rest of his long body with a white glow. Perhaps it was simply the sun's angle, but in places, the light almost seemed to shimmer on his skin as it would off scales. His features were sharp but magnetic. Even from as far away as he stood, she could discern the bright color of his cat eyes and their hunger. She could not fail to notice his erect cock, either.

Allorah averted her eyes, covering herself as best she could. She sat in the water to make her task more manageable.

"I told you I was just going to bathe." She said.

"So, you did." He replied evenly.

When he continued to stare at her, she glanced at him again. "Do you intend to stand there much longer?"

He cocked his head slightly, smiling. "Perhaps. Why?"

She wrapped her arms tighter around her chest as she started to shiver. The combination of inactivity and the water's chill was finally getting to her. "Because it is rather cold in here." She hinted.

But instead of turning away, he started walking into the pool with her. Allorah jumped to her feet, alarmed. The sudden move made her slip on a smooth stone, and she would have fallen if not for Varyn's hand catching her. He steadied her, then began to pull her toward him.

"Wh-what are you doing?" She squeaked.

He pulled her close and wrapped his arms around her. The sensation of his warm, naked flesh coming in contact with her own chilled body set her nerves afire. "Warming you."

She squirmed and pressed her palms against his chest, trying to push him away. "I don't want—" She began.

"Why do you fight me, Allorah?" His voice was soft, insistent.

She glared at him, meeting his eyes even though she knew it was likely a mistake. They had turned a beautiful golden-green color, like afternoon sunlight on new growth, and the pupils seemed to be slightly pointed at the top and bottom. "I don't much like being bewitched." She growled.

His mouth curled in amusement. "I did not bewitch you, Allorah."

"I didn't say you did."

"Then you are referring to the spell?"

"Yes. It has to be." She shoved her against his chest again. "Now let me go!"

"The spell did not bewitch you either." She stopped struggling for a minute to look at him doubtfully.

"Then what did?"

He shrugged and let one of his hands trail gently down her spine. She sucked in a breath. "You were not bewitched at all."

She felt warmth and pleasure following in the wake of his hand, but she ignored them. " Then what do you call this?" She demanded.

"This?" He smiled wickedly. "This is something altogether different."

As his hand dropped to her womanhood, she became highly aware of his erection pressing into her belly. Allorah renewed her efforts to get free. This was getting out of hand. He pulled her closer, dipping his head to nuzzle her neck. One of his long fingers found its way inside her, and she gasped. She was tender down there from last night's activities, but the contact of his hand reawakened the fire he had kindled, and she felt herself weakening under the assault of desire.

"W-why are you doing this to me?" She whimpered.

"Because, my beautiful Priestess," he murmured, his breath warm at her ear, "We are bound, you and I."

"Bound?" Her voice quivered with repressed sensation.

He pressed another finger inside, and she had to bite her lip to keep from moaning. Her fingers curled unconsciously against his chest. "Yes. For we are spellsworn."

She opened her mouth again, but he caught her jaw between his fingers and made her look into his eyes. "No more questions." And he sealed her mouth with his own.

Whatever she had been about to say flew from her mind as she was lost in the hungry dance of tongues and teeth and lips. He used alternately gentle and forceful strokes of his tongue and a steady pumping of his fingers in and out of her to break down her last resistances until she was plaint in his arms.

When he finally broke the kiss, she sighed at a loss. She dreamily stretched up on tiptoe, trying to capture his lips again, but he kept his face teasingly out of reach, close enough to feel his breath but not quite touching. In frustration, she slid her hands from his chest up to his neck, intending to hold him in place, but he removed his fingers from her pussy and caught her wrists quickly. She whined softly in protest and bucked her hips against his leg. He merely smiled and kissed her lightly before using his grip on her arms to turn her around.

Allorah could feel how hard he was against the small of her back. One of his hands was now pressed firmly against her abdomen, while the other kept her arms tucked close to her chest. Her sensitive nipples were being pressed against her forearms at every breath, and this new stimulation made her grind back into him. Gods, she wanted him.

Abruptly, Varyn let go of her wrists and grabbed the base of his cock. He used his other hand to still her wiggling and to keep her at the right angle as he guided himself to her entrance. For a moment, they both paused, relishing the charge of the moment, before he slowly slid all of himself inside her.

Once again, she felt the pleasurably painful sensation of being stretched to capacity. He fit within her so perfectly, so closely, that she could feel his heartbeat throbbing against her walls from his cock. His now free hand rose to her breast, where he rolled the nipple between his fingers. He waited like that for a few breaths, letting her take in the tide of feeling, then began slowly rocking in and out. This new angle made him rub almost constantly against a highly sensitive spot on the front of her pussy walls, and it quickly had her moaning in dizzied pleasure.

The hand on her breast slipped across her chest to pinch and roll her other nipple while his right hand trailed down to where they were joined. With an ease that usually comes with long familiarity, he found her clit and gently pinched that too. Allorah cried out wordlessly. He began rubbing in time with his thrusts, tormenting her inside and out.

The barrage of sensations and the slow pace were driving her wild. In a haze of desire, she reached as far back as she could with one arm and grabbed his hip, trying to pull him further inside. She arched her back wantonly, pressing her breasts into his arm, and pushed her pelvis back into him. She was rewarded as he thrust in a little harder. Her shallow breath hitched and released with a sighing whimper.

As if this was the signal he needed, Varyn picked up speed, keeping the out-strokes leisurely and sensual, but driving in hard. Every time he shoved in, it put delicious pressure on that special place inside her, and she let out a small cry. His rubbing on her button got faster, he pinched her nipple harder. Allorah felt the swirling heat of her pleasure coalescing to the imminent explosion of her climax and knew he was growing close as well. There was a low growl rumbling in his chest, and his breathing was as ragged as her own.

As they drew nearer to their mutual release, his pace quickened further. He began driving in and out with a ferocity that reminded her of last night, and she clutched his arm desperately. Her nails dug into his skin, and his grip on her breast grew painful, but they didn't care. She came suddenly, and she was unprepared for the magnitude of it. It was as if a golden flare detonated in her middle, rushing outward to her extremities in tingles that were charged with lightning. She felt herself arch against him, then go limp as her pussy clenched again and again around his wonderful, powerful cock. And as strong as he was, he could hold out no longer. Allorah felt him swell and throb inside her as his liquid warmth hit her womb. In the one part of her, that was not focused on the squeezing spasms of her core, she was grateful for the strength of his arms holding her up, else she surely would have fallen.

They both came back down slowly, winded and trembling with the aftermath of their ecstasy. Allorah gradually became aware of their surroundings again. They still stood in the middle of the little pool, and the waterfall poured down gently with its soothing, constant sound. Varyn breathed hard against her back, and his arms around her were warm in contrast to the cold of the water. The sun had not changed; though it had seemed an age, it could not have been more than ten minutes they had spent in the realm of passion.

And as her sense of the real world returned, so did the logical mind, with all its condemnations and disapproval. She had done it again and coupled with this man who she barely knew. And if he was to be believed, there had been no enchantment to make her do anything. It had been her own doing. She thought she ought to feel ashamed, but the intensity of her orgasm had drained her, and all she felt was a sort of resignation.

Allorah let her arms fall to her sides, then, when Varyn showed no sign of releasing her on his own, she gently pried his arm from around her chest and lifted his other hand from her loins. As she stepped away somewhat awkwardly, she felt him slide from inside her and was surprised by how empty she felt without him. She tried to distract herself from the feeling by quickly rinsing herself again under the falls and then wading out of the pool to dry off. She realized belatedly that the only thing she had with which to dry herself was her sheer robe.

Sighing, Allorah sat down on the grassy bank. She'd been naked all morning, and he'd already seen —and touched— all there was to see. Fifteen minutes more nakedness wouldn't hurt. He strode out of the water as well and sat down beside her. Close, but not touching. To keep her gaze from wandering to him, she began finger-combing her wet hair.

"What did you mean by 'spells worn?'" She eventually asked.

He stretched languidly and lay back, his hands resting behind his head. "There was an ancient pact between our two peoples, you know. My kind swore to always come to your aid when called. And in return, your people gave their promise to be the guardians and caretakers of this land, for it holds great importance to both our worlds."

"The ritual you performed," he continued, "The summoning is the manifestation of that agreement. Just as our two peoples are bound by the promise our ancestors made, so are you and I bound individually to one another by the spell itself."

"So, I was bewitched!" She cried.

"No. It is not that sort of spell." He rolled his head to the side and looked at her intently. "Think of it more as a marriage of sorts."

She stared at him for a moment. His eyes were lit by a golden fire, and the pupils were more than slightly pointed now. It reminded her of a question that had been bothering her since she'd first seen him, and she used it as a way of changing the unsettling direction of the conversation.

"If you are a dragon, why do you look so human?"

He smiled. "Because you are human. I did not wish to frighten you away with my natural form."

She narrowed her eyes. "So, this is a mere disguise."

"It is an aspect of myself; there is no falsehood in it. This form is as much me as my more... intimidating appearances."

"Show me, then."

His expression grew serious. "Perhaps later." He said and rose to his feet. He offered his hand to her. "We should go. I have an enemy to rout."

Allorah looked at his hand, then scooped up her robe and stood alone. She was afraid to touch him again, lest she was overtaken by the mysterious power he had over her. When they'd sat, she had grown dry enough to don the robe, which she did hastily. She kept her eyes from his and gestured for him to follow her as she went back to the glade.

It was a quick process to gather up what tools she had used for the ritual the night before and put out the smoldering remains of the fire. She had Varyn keep the cat skin and use it as something to wrap around his nudity. He looked amused at her insistence but tied it cleverly around his waist and helped her carry some of the other items. The remaining wax lines were scuffed away, and the incantation of completion was said. The last logs, they left.

When they had finished, Allorah looked around the now-peaceful glade and, sighing, turned to lead them home.

CHAPTER 2

Pausing a moment to sweep a stray curl out of her face with the back of her hand, Allorah briefly scanned the hall. Most of the rectangular space was taken up with the rows of pallets on either side, nearly all occupied by injured men. It was the largest room in the village, originally built for the assembly of the Council of Elders and designed to hold a throng of spectators. At the moment, however, it served as a makeshift hospital. There had to be at least fifty men here, but Allorah felt a swell of pride knowing she had already checked on and treated more than half of them. Dannonae was busy caring for the other half, and soon they would be able to leave matters in the hands of one of the more medically skillful village women and go back home for some much-needed rest.

She was bone-weary and frequently smothered yawns, irritably blinking away the moisture when her eyes watered in reaction. It seemed amazing to her that her eyes could still feel so grainy, even with all the yawn-induced tears.

Bending back to her current patient, she finished wrapping the new dressing around his thigh and tied it off adeptly. Allorah closed her eyes and murmured a short prayer for his fast recovery. When she opened them again, the man was looking up at her, a grateful smile on his mouth.

"Thank you, Allorah. You are surely a blessing sent to us from the Gods."

Allorah made a gentle tsking noise but smiled down at him. "You're too kind, Kalo. I am merely doing my job."

His expression turned more serious. "Still, you do so much. Perhaps too much. You mustn't push yourself too hard."

"I won't." She told him. He didn't look convinced.

"Promise a poor, wounded man that you will care for yourself?" He looked so pitiful that Allorah couldn't help but chuckle and nod her assent.

"I promise. I am nearly finished here, and then I will rest a while."

With a contented sigh, he relaxed back into his pillow, and Allorah patted his wrist and rose to her feet. She carefully concealed the dizzy wave that swept over her before moving to the next man needing her attention.

It was over an hour more before she was through. The torches had been lit to ward off the encroaching gloom of evening, and the sounds of people readying the communal fire drifted up through the branches. Even with the constant danger from the invaders, the townsfolk had deemed fireside time so essential to maintaining and reinforcing their bonds as a community that they risked it every night. The only change was the absence of those Hunters assigned as sentries at posts all around the village. If the foreigners attempted an attack, they would warn those around the fire in time to get them to safety.

Allorah stretched and rolled her shoulders. Her eyes roamed over the resting men until they alighted on Varyn. Dannonae had somehow found him a set of clothes that mostly fit, though the knee-length shirt was a little tight over his broad shoulders, and the trousers were just short. They had not found any boots that would accommodate his large feet, so he went without, but he didn't seem to mind, and it was close enough to work until they came up with something better. So garbed, he had opted to join the two of them as they went about their healing duties, though he made no move to help. Instead, he had occupied himself by talking quietly with those men who were alert enough to do so. Allorah had caught wisps of their conversations, and it seemed he was questioning them closely about the martial abilities of the enemy. Since it seemed to bring a certain level of comfort to the man, she was glad he had found something to do other than watch her because she was worried that his gaze would cause stray thoughts of their recent encounter to surface and distract her.

Her body still seemed to thrum with physical memory of it, though her demanding afternoon had buried the effect somewhat. But every time she looked in his direction, a faint pulse echoed from her core, reminding her. A soft throb came from her aching nether region just thinking about it. It made her want to reach down there and massage the ache out...

Allorah realized the direction of her thoughts with a start and hid her blush by turning away from the room to collect her healing items. She must be more tired than she'd thought to be thinking such things.

As she turned back to the room with renewed composure, Dannonae stood from what she was doing and made her way over. "We've both done enough for one day, I think. You are going home, then?"

"I thought I'd first stop by the fire and perhaps bring the Warrior with me." She replied. "Maybe his presence will bring people some hope."

Dannonae nodded. "Good idea. And if him being there doesn't reassure them, your presence certainly will." Allorah frowned slightly in question. Dannonae smiled. "It is the nature of being a Priestess, my dear. People see you as not only a spiritual leader but a figure they can draw comfort from and rally to in times of distress. Your strength gives them strength in turn." "I hear your words..." She said slowly. "But surely they don't yet see me that way?"

"Of course they do." Dannonae asserted. "They saw you as a Priestess from the first time you joined them at that fire at the age of fifteen. And that impression has only been strengthened over the years, especially by how you've served since the fighting began."

The old Priestess saw her expression of doubt and told her, "When you go down to the fire tonight, watch them. Notice how they treat you, how they watch you subtly yet attentively. And see what your observations tell you."

Allorah nodded. "Where are you going then? To bed, I hope..." She trailed off, giving the older woman a stern look. Dannonae chuckled.

"Doubt yourself you may, but that expression is the mark of a genuine Priestess! Ah, I've taught you well..." They shared a grin before Dannonae sobered, patting her hand. "I will go to bed this night, I promise. But first, I must pray. I fear with all the commotion over the invaders' newest, boldest move, I may not get another chance anytime close to the full moon."

"Oh. I understand, Mother."

Another pat on her hand and Dannonae turned to go. "Gods be with you, Priestess," Allorah called gently. Dannonae looked over her shoulder, a small smile on her lips.

"And you... Priestess."

Shaking her head bemusedly, Allorah went the opposite way over to Varyn. He watched her approach then politely excused himself from his conversation with one of the patients. He nodded his agreement to join her at a communal fire, and two of them made their way out of the long building and down the ramps to the forest floor.

Under the trees, night came early and quickly, bringing a chill that, coupled with the residual dampness from the storm, made her glad of the blazing warmth of the fire. A large crowd had gathered already, sitting, eating, and talking. As Allorah came into the circle of firelight, people hailed her, letting her through and clearing a seat close to the flames. Because of Dannonae's comments, she was aware of the respectful attention that everyone paid her. Then someone noticed Varyn.

Several men stood quickly, their bodies tense, readying themselves for a fight. Allorah spoke quickly to prevent any violence.

"Everyone! This is the Warrior Varyn. I have brought him here in the hope that he will be able to assist us in our fight against the invaders."

There was quiet for a minute as her words sank in. The men standing, all of whom she saw were Hunters, looked at one another, frowning. She noted, though, that the frowns were more worried than doubtful, and after a moment, they all nodded in Varyn's direction and retook their seats. She silently thanked Dannonae for being right; if these people didn't hold her in high regard, that would not have gone over nearly so well. Conversations resumed slowly, at a quieter level than before. Someone offered Allorah a bowl filled with grilled fish and vegetables and, after a tiny hesitation, handed one to Varyn.

As she ate, she continued to watch the villagers' reactions. There were many covert glances stolen at him, some obvious ones, but all of them seemed to be curious instead of suspicious. As laughter joined the talking, Allorah loosed a little sigh of relief. Things were going to be all right. They would accept him.

She finished eating and merely listened to the community around her. She'd forgotten how much peace she found in simply being here among her people in all her business.

Movement off to the side caught her eye. It was Geldan, seemingly returning from his patrol. A seat was cleared for him, and he was handed a bowl of his own. Several men leaned in to talk to him, and she caught the whisper of "...Warrior."

Geldan didn't look up, saying mildly. "So, I hear. We met earlier today."

A few people looked interested in that and pressed him for details, but he only shrugged casually, declining to discuss it. Allorah caught herself frowning and quickly schooled her features to smoothness. For some reason, his casualness didn't seem right to her. Not after the obstinate suspicion, he's shown that afternoon.

Dusk deepened to true night, and as the last people finished eating, the dishes were taken away. More logs were added to the fire, and the younger children were led off to their beds. The conversations turned to darker themes as people began to talk in earnest.

Geldan waited for a general lull in the conversations to speak up. "So. Warrior." He said, still casual. Silence descended over the crowd. "You're here to help us." Allorah felt her uneasiness deepen. She didn't know where he was going with this, but she had the foreboding impression that it wasn't good. Her feeling intensified a moment later when he said. "But none of us have heard how exactly you intend to do that."

Eyes turned to Varyn for his response. He returned evenly, "That depends on what you want me to do. And what you will allow me to teach you."

"Teach?" Geldan's raised his eyebrows in surprise. "You're going to teach us? What sort of things?"

"I will teach you War."

Geldan looked around as whispers flitted through the crowd. "That's an awfully broad topic, Warrior... Certainly, you can give us something more specific?"

"The first thing I will teach you is tactics." He told them, his green gaze steady on Geldan. "As a hunting people, you fight well enough, but your use of the territory is pathetic. This is your land; you know it better than anyone. Doubtless better than these invaders, yet you don't use that to your advantage."

Anger flashed across Geldan's expression before he returned it to a strained neutral. "And you think you can do better?"

"I know it."

"How do you know it? Where does all this knowledge come from anyway?" He was rapidly losing his calm fa9ade, his voice growing heated.

"Geldan..." Allorah said lowly, warningly.

"And being so knowledgeable, of course, you already know that there hasn't been a Warrior on this island for over a century because there haven't been any wars! This means that wherever you gained your Warrior skills, it wasn't here. Coincidentally, the only people who seem to know as much about war as you do, are the invaders trying to kill us all!" He had dropped all pretenses now and was openly glaring. "I say you're one of them!"

"That is enough!" Allorah snapped, rising to her feet. "This man is our ally, Hunter, and I will not have you abuse him so!" Geldan stood too.

"With all due respect, Allorah, how can you know for certain? Of course, he claims to be an ally. A Warrior even!" His tone dripped with ridicule. "But have you any proof? Have you ever actually seen him kill a foreigner?"

Allorah opened her mouth to upbraid him for his intolerable rudeness, then stopped as she realized she hadn't seen anything supporting Varyn's claims... Yes, his eyes were strange, but that alone wasn't enough to reveal anything, and there was no actual evidence to prove his skill. Or his allegiance. Her mouth tightened in frustration. "No." She answered grudgingly.

A triumphant gleam lit his eyes, and he pressed his advantage, sensing her inner debate. "Exactly. There is only his word for any of it." Ominous muttering rippled through the spectators. Geldan seemed to take encouragement from it, and his next comment was directed partially at them. "Only his word that he will not lead the invaders here to murder us in our beds!" The mutters rose to an angry buzz directed at Varyn.

"Careful, Hunter." She with dangerous softness. The crowd immediately went dead silent. "This is the second time today you have disputed the information I have already accepted as truth. Any further accusations I will take as a personal affront. When you question his word, you question mine."

Geldan's eyes widened; he seemed to flounder for some way to respond. The quietly powerful voice of Varyn saved him from having to. "He is right, though."

It was Allorah's turn for a shock as all eyes turned to him in inquiry. He gave a crooked smile. "I have shown you nothing yet to merit your trust. And as you are under attack, your refusal to give it unconditionally is only to be expected. I will have to provide you with proof of my legitimacy."

"And how do you propose to do that?" Geldan asked nastily. He seemed to have regained his speech.

Varyn did not respond to the tone. "You spoke today of the threat of invaders in the woods nearby." He stared calmly at Geldan. "I will remove that threat."

Several of the Hunters around the fire made loud scoffing noises. One of them, who Allorah didn't know the name of, spoke up. "Don't you think we tried that? There are too many of them to attack. Too fierce. And we haven't the men to be able to afford such a maneuver."

Varyn looked unfazed. "I intend to go alone. Tonight."

This time there was a much louder outburst of exclamations and protests. Geldan looked as though he had something to say, but he kept his mouth closed after a glance at Allorah. The same man as before spoke again, incredulous. "That is suicide; I don't care how good you claim to be. And even if it wasn't... How can we know you don't go rendezvous with them if you go alone?" Allorah glared at him in a warning and quickly added, "But if you insist on following through with such insanity, someone should at least go with you. If only to tell us all how you died." There was quite a moment as they waited for Varyn's reply.

"That is the one thing you must trust me about." He said slowly. "I go alone." He rose from his seat, and in the orange illumination of the flames, he looked genuinely daunting. "You will have your proof." And he turned and walked into the dark.

Voices were raised in conversation and questions. Several of the Hunters rose as well and made as if to follow, but Allorah halted them with a look and went after him on her own. She caught up to him quickly and grabbed his wrist to pull him to a stop. Her eyes were still adjusting to the night away from the fire, but she could see his emerald gaze glowing down at her with a hint of golden light.

"You don't have to do this, you know." She told him. "There are other ways."

"But what did you summon me for, if not this?"

"I certainly didn't summon you to die!" She said sharply.

She felt, more than saw, his smile. "Could it be that you are worried for my safety?" He asked teasingly. Allorah said nothing. "Never fear, my lovely one. It would take much more than a few mere humans to feel me. I will return."

The almost arrogant confidence of his tone both exasperated and reassured her. She sighed. "When?"

"When I am finished." He bent and took her lips in a slow, firm kiss that left her wanting. His mouth curled in a smug little smile as they parted. "Go back home, Allorah. Sleep."

Her mouth twisted wryly. "Not likely. But I'll go home anyway." The smile slipped away, and she searched what she could discern of his features through the dark. "Be careful." She murmured.

His hand cupped her cheek, thumb trailing along her lips. Then he stepped back and turned to disappear into the shroud of nighttime. She blinked. One moment she saw him; the next didn't, though she thought she should have been able to see some trace of light reflection off his remarkable silver hair. But there was nothing. She peered around her for a moment more, listening, and detected only the quiet forest sounds and those of the people around the fire. Perhaps he would be able to manage this after all...

She returned briefly to the fire to bid everyone a good night before beginning the walk up to the treetops and then to her home at the eastern edge of the village. It was only when she was halfway up the ramp to the house that she realized Varyn had taken no weapon.

Halting immediately, she turned to go back down, then paused. She anxiously caught her bottom lip between her teeth. He was certainly long gone by now. There was nothing she could do, but it made her almost physically ill to think of him completely alone in such grave danger, without even a dagger to defend himself. She told herself to calm down. Trust that he knew what he was doing. And if he were a dragon, what difference would having a man-made weapon make anyway?

It didn't help. Panic constricted her chest.

Allorah made herself start walking back up the ramp again. Even breaths. She tried to distract herself from the gruesome thoughts by analyzing her reaction. Why should she care so much? Her fear was far too real to attempt dismissing it as simple concern for the potential loss of an ally, and she certainly wasn't afraid he would betray her people. So why? The answer loomed starkly in front of her, but she shied away from acknowledging it, even as she accepted its truth. She wasn't sure why she avoided even thinking about it, except that it filled her with a different sort of fright.

She walked the rest of the way up, trying to think of nothing.

Sitting outside on her little balcony, she pulled the shawl closer around her bare shoulders and looked up at the stars. She thought of trying to count them all to ease her worry. She knew both tasks were impossible. Instead, she settled for picking out the constellations, reciting each one's story to herself under her breath.

There was the fish, swimming through the inky waters in the endless search for his brother on another side of the sky. The tree under whose sparkling branches reclined the maiden and whose far-reaching roots touched the back of the mole. And there was the cat, ever hunting the unsuspecting bird with its magnificent, twinkling plumage. There was the dragon...

The dragon.

Constellations were not that interesting after all, she decided. Definitely not worth freezing herself for. Allorah stood up from the bench and went inside, closing the door firmly behind her.

To keep the candles from being blown out, she unrolled the woven cloth draperies to cover her windows before entering the main room. Maybe some sedative tea would let her fall asleep. She sat at the table while she waited for the water to heat, unconsciously twisting the corner of her shawl between anxious fingers. Out of the corner of her eye, she saw the panel of the hidden entrance to the room below swing open, and Dannonae stepped out. Allorah didn't look over but continued thinking about the cloth between her fingers. Seeing her distraction, the old Priestess went over to the stove and looked at the jar Allorah had taken out for her tea.

"Valerian root?" She murmured in tones of surprise, glancing at her former apprentice. "Has something happened?"

Allorah didn't look up but spoke curtly. "He's gone to rout the invaders in the Sacred Wood."

"Oh." She said.

The kettle started to hiss, and Dannonae took it off the flame, pouring the steaming water into a cup. She sprinkled in a careful dose of the herb, then set the mixture in front of Allorah, seating herself at the corner next to her and folding her hands on the tabletop. Allorah didn't touch the cup, and Dannonae didn't say anything, merely watched the younger woman absorbed in her thoughts. Abruptly she spoke.

"I am a fool."

Dannonae raised an eyebrow. "Why do you say that?"

Allorah's mouth twisted in a self-mocking smile. "He is a dragon. I know that. Of course, he's capable of taking care of himself. And the whole reason why I brought him here was to help us fight those horrible people. Yet... Now that he's out there..." She saw a knowing smile on Dannonae's face and looked at her sharply. "What?"

"Perhaps you are being a little irrational, Allorah, but you have never been a fool. Even as a child, you possessed wisdom beyond your years." Her eyes held a parent's warmth as she gently removed the mangled cloth from Allorah's fingers. She looked as though she were about to say something more for a moment, then she sighed and looked away.

She rose from her seat, using her hands to leverage her to stand. Allorah noticed sadly that this past year had not been kind to her mentor; she seemed to age visibly every day. Dannonae gave her another smile and affectionately brushed a hand over her hair. "Drink your tea."

Allorah smiled weakly back and picked up the cup. Satisfied, Dannonae turned and went into her room, shutting the door quietly.

Allorah watched the closed door for a minute, then stood as well. Taking small sips of the hot liquid so as not to scald her tongue, she went to her own room. She turned down the covers on her bed while she waited for the brew to cool, then combed the silken tumble of hair that fell to the middle of her back. She washed her face and used the remaining water and a cleansing paste to scrub her teeth with a small, stiff brush. Once her ablutions were completed, she gulped down the remaining tea, blew out the candles, and climbed into bed.

Curled in the comfort of her familiar blankets, and with the sedative now in her system, she should have been able to fall asleep. The barely perceptible swaying of the great tree had always been lulling to her before, and the soft rustle of the leaves had accompanied her to slumber for many years. Yet she twisted uncomfortably in her bed, unable to quiet her thoughts long enough for unconsciousness to overtake her.

Finally, she threw aside the blankets in disgust and sat on the edge of the bed. Her night-adjusted eyes wandered restlessly around the little room until they descended upon the fur lying on the chest at the foot of her bed. It was the cat pelt that she'd used for the ritual. The one that Varyn had worn.

She didn't know what made her do it, but she reached over and picked it up, bringing it close to her and inhaling. Mostly she smelled the slightly musty smell familiar to furs, but there... very faintly, was something else—the trace of a strange, masculine scent lingering on the pelt. Allorah breathed in again, then climbed back under the covers, spreading the fur on top. She rustled around a little but stilled after a minute.

There, with the hint of him near her, she finally drifted off to sleep.

Allorah Dreamed. She knew instinctively that this was no mere fantasy but something more. It had happened to her frequently when she was younger, these strange dreams that were not dreams, sometimes even when she was awake. Dannonae called them visions. Sometimes they felt like memories, though not hers. At other times they had the ephemeral quality that led her to believe they were events yet to occur.

This time, she saw it as if it was happening.

The coiled figure stalked his prey in deadly silence, gliding along the darkened forest with all the substance of a moon-cast shadow. He carried no weapons, nor did he need any. The two men he hunted, their pale eyes wide with fear, kept close to one another. Moonlight glinted off the swords they held in trembling hands and off their fair hair; they twitched and tensed at the small nighttime sounds around them. The figure grinned in feral delight.

In a flicker of movement, he was behind the one to the left. He gripped his victim's head between his hands and twisted. With a quiet "pop," the man dropped like a stone, his neck broken. The figure disappeared again before the second man finished turning toward the sound. He let out a strangled gasp and whipped around again, brandishing his sword around him in wild terror.

The figure watched his flailing prey from the shadows off to the side. He contemplated finishing him, putting him out of his misery, then decided against it. It better to discretely herd him to one of the other, larger pockets of men, where his wild-eyed tale about annihilating his unit would plant the seed of fright in the others. It would expedite the process of spooking them out of their conditioning and meticulous organization, leaving them in the vulnerable mentality of the hunted and making them that much easier to kill.

As the figure began luring his prey to his decided destination, using little sounds to spur the panicked man in the right direction, a small part of the Dreaming Allorah registered this most unusual ability to hear the hunter's thoughts. In all her visions up until now, she had only served as an outside observer, never actually privy to what any of the participants were thinking. The abnormality was quickly tucked away for later, and her full attention returned to the scene.

For hours the figure continued his deadly game. Even after slowly picking off all the members of the group he'd led the unfortunate soldier to, he moved to the next and began again. Sometimes he killed them all; other times, he spared a few to stumble upon his next targets, where they were usually included in the ensuing slaughter anyway. But the overall strategy was always in his mind, so he carefully let one from every third group or so flee back to the rest of their army. The combination of their separate testimonies should have the effect of dissuading their commanders from attacking through these woods again.

He mostly used his hands to do the work, fingernails extended and hardened to wicked claws. It was as much Shifting as he would allow himself. To go any further would remove all challenges from the encounters. And there was a sort of pleasure in excelling within these self-imposed limitations.

The slightest lightening in the patches of sky visible through the trees told him it was time to finish up. There was one more group he wanted to deal with before he did, though. Slipping through the undergrowth, a little smile curved his lips when he saw all the soldiers crouched and intently looking toward the village. His smile widened when he saw the ornamentation on a soldier's sword in the middle of the group. An officer...

Without warning, he leaped from his cover and attacked. His claws ripped through one man's throat; a kick sent splinters of bone into another's brain. He moved so quickly that three more died before the rest realized what was happening. They sluggishly attempted a counter-attack, and the figure relished the variation in the routine. Subtlety had its place and purpose, but a direct approach was much more satisfying. Easily dodging their weapons, he picked up one of the swords from the ground and began wielding it to deadly effect. The officer swung at him, screaming in rage, and the figure knocked the blow aside, continuing the motion to run one of the other soldiers through.

Moments later, only the officer was left. He breathed heavily in fear or fury, though the figure was not winded. A flurry of activity and the officer's ornamented sword were in the other man's hand. It was time to return to the village, and the officer would be coming with him. Turning him around by sword-point, he prodded him in the back, and they began walking.

Allorah flew to consciousness with a start.

The images from her vision tumbled and tangled in her mind as she threw off the covers and fumbled in the pre-dawn gloom for her shawl, but one thought dominated all the others: Varyn was back. She delayed running out the door only long enough to pull on and hastily lace her midcalf boots. Her ebon curls streamed unbound as she raced down the spiraling ramp to the main level of the village and the cold air chilled her face, bringing a pink flush to her cheeks.

Nearly all the torches had been extinguished, and the moon had long since set. But it didn't matter to her. She knew where she was going as if a string tied around her heart was tugging her in the right direction. She flew along the wooden paths, one hand barely keeping the shawl from blowing away in her haste. Aside from her footfalls' light, rapid cadence, the still-dark morning was utterly silent until a piercing whistle shrilled from a distance. It was a sentry's warning of someone's approach.

She skidded to a stop at the very edge of the treetop pathways. She braced her hands on the railing, leaning forward over the border to peer into the shrinking darkness below. There was nothing. Behind her, armed men rushed from their homes in response to the sentry's call. She heard confused murmurs as they saw her standing there, then she saw it. A small patch of silver moved towards them on the forest floor.

Her breath caught in her throat, and she sped to the nearest lift. Two men stepped inside before she could close the gate to go down, and she clenched her jaw impatiently as one of them kept their descent to a safely slow pace. By the time they reached the ground, it was clear that two figures were approaching, one in front of the other.

An image of the officer in her dream flashed through her head, making her blink and pause, momentarily disoriented. Regaining her senses, she saw the men who'd come down with her raising their bows to aim at the figures who walked toward them.

"No!" She cried. She darted forward to place her body between them and the oncoming men. "Do not shoot!"

They exchanged a startled glance and looked at her as if to say something. A sudden thought occurred to her, and she ran far enough out from under the treetop walkways that by squinting, she could barely make out the drawn bows of the defenders above. Fear gave her voice strength as she screamed desperately to them, "DO NOT SHOOT!"

Miraculously, they heard, and she saw one man raise his hand to signal that all should wait. Allorah let her anxious breath leave her and turned back to the forest. She could see Varyn's face and that of the bearded officer he had captured. She was looking him over for injury when the two men from the lift, two new ones, and Geldan all appeared at her elbow. They waited with her silently as Varyn closed the remaining distance and forced the officer to his knees before them.

After a moment, Geldan said, almost as if he couldn't believe it, "You're alive."

"I am," Varyn added, smiling, "And I've brought you all a gift." He poked the kneeling officer in the shoulder with one sword, and the man flinched, lowering his head. Geldan and the others looked at him in bewilderment.

"What are we supposed to do with him?" He asked, only confusion in his voice.

Varyn shrugged. "Whatever you like. If you decide to kill him, I advise questioning him first."

Geldan nodded slowly. With a graceful movement, Varyn flipped the sword in his left hand around so that he held it by the blade and offered it hilt-first to the shorter man while he kept the officer in place by pressing the ornamented sword's point into the back of his neck. Geldan took the sword gingerly but gave a respectful nod before motioning for two others to hoist the officer to his feet and bear him away. After another glance at Varyn, he and the other two turned to follow, leaving Allorah alone with him.

She could only look at him for a minute. His hands and arms were stained crimson, and blood spotted his torso, but she felt no alarm. She asked anyway. "Are you injured?"

One side of his mouth curled up in a crooked smile. "No." "Then all that blood—?" "Is not mine." He finished for her. She nodded in affirmation of her own thoughts.

"Come." She told him, turning away. "We will get you cleaned up."

As she led him back up the lift and along the walkways, eyes, and whispers of the emerging townsfolk following them, she felt a fluttering in her stomach that was mingled relief and something else. She didn't dwell on it.

Her tower home was too far for practicality, so they went into the first of the communal kitchen buildings they came across. At this time in the morning, no one was inside, so they were alone. She went to one of the rain barrels and filled a bowl for him to wash. When she turned back, he had already removed his scarlet-soaked shirt and deposited his similarly drenched sword on the table. As she silently handed him the bowl and a rag to scrub with, she took a moment to marvel again at the masculine beauty of his body. The blood streaking his chest and arms seemed to heighten it, adding an initial roughness to his sculpted perfection. Unconsciously, she wetted her lips with the tip of her tongue.

He washed quickly while she waited. She felt herself filling with a strange sort of calm in just watching him, hale, whole, and preoccupied. And that moment, she allowed her mind to touch on the depth of her feeling for him, even if only for a heartbeat. She loved him. No matter how suddenly it had happened, no issue that she hardly knew him. She loved him...

Allorah stepped forward, close enough that she was sure he could feel her breath warming the water on his chest. She reached up with one hand and gently turned his face towards her. The surprise she found there made her smile. She'd caught him off-balance. Then she stood on tip-toe and pulled his mouth down to hers.

The kiss didn't start passionate, but it soon became so. The banked fire within both their bodies flared brightly, burning for completion. She parted her lips and opened her eyes to look at him dazedly. "I'm glad you're back."

He kissed her again, hard. "I told you I would be."

"Yes, you did..." And other words were lost as he brought her close and resumed where they had left off. She felt him swelling against her abdomen with an answering slickness gathering between her legs. Suddenly she pulled away again, murmuring, "No..."

He stopped immediately but frowned down at her in confusion. "No?"

A wicked gleam lit her violet eyes as she grabbed his hands around her waist and began tugging him after her. "Not here." She walked backward, leading him to the storage room door for the kitchen supplies. Catching on to her intention, he kicked the door closed behind them and followed her until her back bumped into the far wall. Then it was a frenzy of activity as they rushed to bare themselves enough to be joined. Her shawl dropped to the floor, discarded, and she quickly wriggled out of her lower undergarments, not having worn anything to bed. His dexterous fingers quickly unlaced his trousers, and as his impressive length sprang free, he sighed gratefully.

"I have a newfound respect for human males..." He muttered, gripping her waist again, lifting her effortlessly into the air. Realizing his aim, Allorah hiked up her shift enough to allow her to encircle his waist with her legs, and she wrapped her arms around his neck. He used his grasp on her hips to line himself up with her entrance, coating the tip with his juices. Then he dropped her.

She gave a muffled cry as she sank, sheathing him fully. Her inner walls rippled at the welcome intrusion, so much sudden stimulation all at once. His hands shifted from their position on her hips to grab her bottom, slowly lifting her again. As she moaned at the sensation of his flesh dragging out of hers, she relished the possessive power of his hands squeezing through the thin material. Then he let her sink back down again, and they started all over.

He soon got into a rhythm, and she discovered she could add enormous pleasure by circling her hips while he was buried deep inside her. She did this on every other downstroke until her head was reeling, and she could only moan while he bounced her up and down on his cock. Her nipples were like little pebbles, constantly rubbed by the weave of her shift as she pressed her chest to his. His mouth found her neck, and he licked and bit along the ivory skin. The scrape of his teeth and his fingers digging into her cheeks as he ravished her vigorously sent her over the edge. She smothered her yelled against his shoulder and bucked hard against him, wanting to feel him let go as well. At the end of her climax, she squeezed him with her pussy muscles as hard as she could, clenching him to a halt. He gasped, and with the tiny jerk of her hips, she felt him swell and explode, coating her walls with sticky warmth and sending tingling aftershocks throughout her system. He threw back his head and groaned, and Allorah watched the pleasure on his face with satisfaction. He was magnificent.

After a moment, he began calming his breaths, and he tilted his head forward again and grinned lopsidedly at her. She smiled back and leaned in to press her lips to his briefly, then stared contentedly at the gold swirling through the green of his irises. He brought her out of her study by returning the kiss quickly before carefully lifting her off his softening length and letting her slide down to the floor. Allorah sighed resignedly at a loss but looked around for where she'd dropped her undergarment while he tucked himself back in and began lacing up.

A minute later and they were both decent again, though Allorah was conscious of the lingering flush of exertion in her cheeks, and Varyn still wore a self-satisfied smile. Leading the way back into the kitchen, Allorah cleaned up the washing tools and the table, and Varyn picked up his bloodied shirt with a mostly clean part. He used it to clean the sword's hilt before picking it up. The sight of the blood sobered her a little, a reminder that he had spent the night killing.

But she didn't let it bother her too much, and she turned her thoughts to other things she had more influence over. Such as his diet. He didn't look tired, but she thought he surely must be hungry by now. The kitchen was still empty save for the two of them, so that no hot meals would be coming out of there for a while, but there was food at her home, and while he ate, maybe they could try doing something about either washing that shirt or getting him a new one...

Voices and footsteps came from the walkway outside. She realized now that he'd proved his authenticity, the Hunters and the other fighters would all want to speak with him about the war, making plans and learning what he had to teach. She'd only just discovered that she wanted him to herself, and now everyone else would want some of his time too. The irony made her sigh again.

Varyn looked at her inquisitively, but she merely shrugged and smiled to indicate it was nothing. The footsteps stopped outside the kitchen door as if they hesitated to interrupt. Allorah ignored them. "Are you hungry?" She asked.

"I am." He replied.

"Good." She started walking toward the door, and he followed. "I believe there is some stew left over at my home."

"Perfect."

She opened the door, and sure enough, several Hunters stood outside, looking expectant. Allorah nodded politely at them and walked right past, Varyn at her side. She caught a glimpse of their faces as she passed, surprise and respect mixed. A little smile curved her lips, and she kept on walking.

The rest of the world could wait for a while.

THE END